Molly McBride and the Plaid Jumper

Text and illustrations by

Jean Schoonover-Egolf

Our Sunday Visitor

Huntington, Indiana

www.osv.com

For my mom, Dolores Joan Born Schoonover.
She always saw the best in me.

24 23 22 21 20 19   2 3 4 5 6 7 8 9

ISBN: 978-1-68192-508-0
LCCN: 2019939995

Our Sunday Visitor Publishing Division
Our Sunday Visitor, Inc.
200 Noll Plaza
Huntington, IN 46750
1-800-348-2440

Molly McBride and Francis tried to hide.

Soon, Molly would start kindergarten at Holy Trinity School. She couldn't wear her favorite purple nun's habit to school . . . only a plaid jumper.

It was the rule!

Molly's friends, the Children of Mary Sisters, wore purple habits. Molly wanted to be just like them, so her Momma had made her a purple habit to wear, too.

She wore it **every single day.**

But now Momma said she had to wear that plaid jumper instead.

Sissy tried to help.

"There, there, Molly. Wearing a school uniform just means you're growing up. Lots of people wear uniforms. Cooks wear uniforms. Police wear uniforms. Jail convicts wear uniforms. And . . ."

". . . Catholic school kids wear uniforms!"

After dinner that night, Molly asked Daddy about her problem.

"Daddy, why can't I wear my purple habit to school? It's Catholic, right? In fact, isn't it even **MORE** Catholic than a jumper?

"And no one will know how special I am if I'm wearing the same thing as everyone else!"

Daddy smiled kindly.

"Molly, honey, school uniforms are what you wear for learning. Your plaid jumper tells everyone that you belong to Holy Trinity Catholic School.

"Why, I'll bet all your friends in the Children of Mary Sisters wore plaid jumpers when they were in school!"

Molly wasn't so sure about that. And she had other worries about this whole starting-kindergarten-thing.

For one thing, Molly had never been apart from Francis, but wolf-pets weren't allowed at school.

She was very concerned about him. "Now Francis, you have got to stop being so shy. I know there's a big, brave wolf inside you!"

"Try to make friends with some of the other toys," she counseled him. "Don't be afraid! Bear and Bunny would love to play with you if you'd just ask. Tomorrow morning, I want you to hop right out of this bed, give them your biggest smile, and just say hello."

But Francis only sighed.

Molly said a little prayer that Francis would learn to see himself as Molly saw him.

The next day, Momma took Molly to school for Orientation Day. On Orientaion Day, kids visited the school to meet the teacher and their classmates.

It was not a *real* school day, so Molly didn't have to wear that plaid jumper.

But when she walked into the school, Molly couldn't believe her eyes. Kids were already wearing their uniforms!

"You know you don't have to wear that thing today, right?" she said to one girl. "This is only an orientation, not real school yet."

Molly sighed. Didn't anyone understand?

But then she saw a boy who was dressed just as specially as she was. He was wearing black pants and a black t-shirt with a long, narrow strip of white paper taped around his neck.

He looked just like a priest!

After the teacher finished talking to the kids, they went out to the playground.

Molly saw that special boy on the swings. She decided to be brave
(just like Francis!). She went right over to the swings and said
hello to the boy.

"What's your name?" she asked politely.

"My name is Dominic," he said shyly, "and I'm going to be a
priest when I grow up."

Molly beamed. "I'm Molly McBride, and I'm going to be a Children of Mary sister when I grow up."

"A Purple Nun!" Dominic exclaimed.

And just like that, Molly had a best friend.

Just then, the teacher called the kids back inside. Molly hoped there wasn't more orienting to do.

Dominic whispered to Molly, "I don't want to wear a school uniform, do you? How can I look like a priest if I'm wearing blue pants and a white shirt?"

"And how can I look like a Purple Nun if I'm wearing a plaid jumper?" Molly agreed.

"I know!" Dominic exclaimed. "We can talk to my special friend, Father Matt. He can help us!"

"Great idea!" Molly exclaimed. "I'll bet he won't make us wear a school uniform, 'cause he knows how important it is for priests and nuns to wear special clothes!"

But when they walked into the classroom, they were surprised to see Father Matt. *Really* surprised . . .

"Great costumes!" he added when he noticed Molly and Dominic.

"But you're not wearing your priest clothes," squeaked Dominic.

The teacher, laughing at the kids' expressions, explained.

"Father Matt has just returned from vacation in Florida, class.
He hasn't had a chance to change out of his beach clothes yet!"

"Uniforms are important!"

everyone had been telling Molly. Was Father
Matt saying they *weren't* important?

"But if you're not dressed like a priest,"
Molly wanted to know, "what if
somebody thinks you're a surfer
guy or something? Wouldn't they
accidentally call you *mister*
instead of *father*?"

The priest smiled.

"It wouldn't change a thing, kids. The day I received the sacrament of Holy Orders, my priestly identity was stamped on me so permanently that nothing, not even a swim in the ocean, can wash it off."

"God can see through all that anyways," Father Matt went on. "He knows who we are and loves us no matter what we're wearing. He sees who we really are inside, and what we are meant to be."

That night, Molly and
Momma laid out clothes for school.
Daddy came in, too, to say good night.
Molly looked at the plaid jumper and thought about
all the new things that had happened that day.

Momma handed her something soft and familiar.
It was her purple bandana.

"Would it make you feel better to wear
your bandana to school?" she asked.
"I checked, and you can."

"Yes!" Molly blurted out happily.

"But you still have to wear your plaid jumper," Daddy said, giving her a little tickle under the chin.

Molly laughed. "That's okay, I think, 'cause you know what? It's the love between Jesus and me that makes me special, more than the clothes. And, anyway, he sees underneath everything. He sees all the way inside us!"

"But special clothes are important, too," she added hurriedly. "They're just not as important as Jesus' love. Because nothing can wash that away, not even an ocean!"

Momma and Daddy laughed. They hugged and kissed
Molly good night.

"Molly McBride," Momma said, "I'm positive
God sees something very special inside you."